A Broken River Books original

Broken River Books
10765 SW Murdock Lane
Apt. G6
Tigard, OR 97224

Interior design by J David Osborne

ISBN: 978-1-940885-09-4

Printed in the USA.

BLACK GUM

J DAVID OSBORNE

BROKEN RIVER BOOKS
PORTLAND, OR

For Matthew Revert
and Steve

“Move as a godless heathen
Black gums, tooth gone”
—Aesop Rock, “Gopher Guts”

I

FIREWORKS

We drove out to Blackgum just east of Muskogee. We parked at the lip of a ditch and got out under clouds too heavy for summer. There on the road she took a picture of me. I had my hands in my pockets and I looked like I was tired of where I stood or any other place I might stand.

My wife and I came out there to see our friend Susan. Her family put on the best fireworks display in Oklahoma. We also came out there because a few days ago my wife told me that I was an angry person and that she needed time alone and I knew the man she'd been texting would be there. We walked over the cattle guard and down the gravel road to the house where Susan's brothers were sorting the fireworks. They had a layout: black cats and M80s and these big motherfuckers you drop down a tube and they shoot up. Her brothers were friendly enough but they didn't really talk and so we sat and watched them set up the fireworks until Susan's mother came out and gathered us and took us inside to eat.

More and more folks arrived and they all ate and drank beers and talked amongst each other and I had no idea where to go or what to do or why I'd been invited to this thing in the first place. The man showed up and pushed his long hair out of his eyes and gave us both a hug. I could have just hit him and the three of us would have known why, but I didn't and so it was just the three of us that went on knowing what we knew.

He and I made small talk and I felt outside of myself, away from the tire swing hanging from the oak tree at the edge of the property. The man too was outside of himself and though we made words and smiled we were the whole time circling each other like dogs.

While Susan's family got the display set up and her sisters got changed, my wife wandered off to pet a llama a hundred yards down the barb wire fence. I watched her lips move and the thing lost interest in her and walked out into the long grass.

Susan and her sisters had set up little platforms out in their front yard and when the clouds were ready to kiss the ground her brothers started up the fireworks. The rain came down and the copper lit the low clouds purple and blue. Susan and her sisters performed a dance. I sat on one side of my wife and the man sat on the other and we watched the spectacle.

When it was over we headed inside. I said I was tired and told Susan and so she showed me to my room. I got in there and she grabbed my wife by the arm and said, "Let me show you where you're sleeping," and I didn't say anything. The door shut.

I lay down and looked at the dolls in the room and I couldn't get comfortable. I'd had a few and my mind was wandering. I heard them in the living room, maybe twenty of them, singing "Jolene," and I got up from the bed and went out there and my wife was sitting by the man, too close.

I told everyone that I was leaving and they said that it was late and that I'd had too much but I just repeated myself. Before I left I saw her and him and she looked at me then looked down at her phone and he looked off into the distance, his thin arms behind him and too close.

I'd always felt a certain inclination to hurt others. Always got a kick out of knocking someone straight. But I didn't do a thing. I just left. The rain had let up and it smelled good outside.

I'd never seen myself as such a boy until that moment, when everything that seemed so big was in fact only a small part of several beginnings, and I drove all the way back to Comanche in tears and I didn't stop til I got to Charlie's and he took me in.

BLEACH

Charlie was a mechanic. At any given point there'd be two hollowed-out Mustangs in his driveway, tranny over here, drivetrain over there. The grass was too long and there were beer cans and cardboard beer boxes and cigarette butts scattered over it. Looked about the same as the rest of the yards in the neighborhood.

The night I showed up he went to his room and came back with niacin capsules filled with speed. I ate mine and chased it with beer.

His living room was a couch and a recliner and stains in the carpet.

We got real high. The icons on my phone screen jiggled. I clenched my teeth.

I felt great.

Charlie said, "Business was great for a little bit but then they stole my shit. Every time. They come by at night and they take from the cars and did you know that now I owe fucking a thousand bucks to this dude? A fucking grand. Fucking niggers just reach in and take shit out the car, I don't even know if they know what it is that they're taking, they just fucking take it. I'm in the hole, now. I was making money and it was okay and now I owe a fucking grand."

I said, "Whoa."

He said, "I just wanted to have my own business, that's all. Worked Hibdon for years and I just wanted to start up my own thing. But now all this. This fucking neighborhood. But I guess that's life in the hood," and he started laughing like crazy.

I looked at my phone and thought, *I am having a great time.*

Charlie leaned forward in the recliner. "You know Ryan's in jail."

"Ryan? No."

"Ryan's in jail. He shot a dude over some bullshit. He's in jail, and Anuky's fighting in the MMA. He does stuff here. Seen him hit a dude so hard the motherfucker went down. He's fighting."

"Ryan shot someone?"

"There was this time my uncle shot a dude and he went to jail for a long time. That shit is crazy. Ryan looked like Eminem. Don't you think Ryan looked like Eminem?"

"He did the bleach."

"Yeah, the fucking bleach. Ryan looked like Eminem. Man I am rolling my fucking tit off."

"Me too." I chewed at my lip.

KITCHEN MESS

Later on, when it was nearly dawn, I was awake and texting every woman in my phone.

I heard Charlie's door open and saw him walk out and look at me. Nothing registered. He had wild hair. He felt around in his pants and whipped his dick out and started pissing into his kitchen.

I watched, and I laughed.

The next morning I had gotten maybe an hour of sleep when Charlie woke me up.

"I ain't gonna be mad," he said. "But did you fucking piss in my kitchen?"

We went and got food and I read all the text messages in my phone. Charlie ate a grilled cheese.

"Sometimes," he said, "I feel like the internet runs my life. I just click stuff. Doesn't matter what it is. I clicked a link the other day, it made me feel bad. It wasn't even weird though, it was just a guy deep-frying a pineapple. It was one of those 'you won't believe what happens' things. But I felt bad about it. After I watched it though, I realized that if a guy came out of an alley holding a pineapple and said 'Wanna see me deep-fry this bitch?' I'd probably say 'hell yeah.'"

After our meal we walked out into the sun and watched the cars pass. A group of older folks in automated wheelchairs camped out at the end of the street.

"You have to eat," Charlie said.

"Not hungry."

"Yeah, me neither. But you have to. Otherwise you'll get strung out."

"What are we doing?"

Charlie checked his watch. "Shane's coming over. You've met my cousin, yeah?"

THE HEATHEN

Shane fashioned knives out of railroad spikes. He gifted one to Charlie wrapped in a paper towel to make it a surprise. He pointed out the duct tape wrapped around the hilt and Charlie stabbed the air with it.

Charlie gifted him a tattoo back. Shane's face and his arms were covered in them, tiny knives and cats and lightning bolts and numbers and names. Tonight he wanted something different. He wanted Charlie to tattoo his gums.

Shane's torso and legs were completely bare. When I asked him why only his arms and face were tattooed, he told me that in the underworld, the ink was all anyone could see. That they glow neon down there. I asked, "But won't you be naked when you die?" and he said, "It's cold in hell. I'm going to be wearing clothes."

I said, "So why tattoo your gums?"

He said, "When I meet the devil, I want him to know that I'm a friendly guy."

I ate two capsules and cringed and watched my friend power up his gun. His foot tapping the pedal.

That sound. When the needle hit the softness above Shane's teeth he howled and when his mouth was full of blood he gurgled.

When it was done we played beer pong with Kentucky Deluxe. I looked down at my phone every time Shane took a drink, his scream caterpillaring up atop the mushroom clouds of Archie Lee bass rattling the small speakers alone on the floor by the stack of magazines.

After Charlie sunk his third shot and Shane hollered again, my friend came around the fold-out picnic table and tilted his cousin's head back, the blurry green tattoos of his hands on Shane's inked face like two warring clouds of gnats. Charlie peeled back Shane's lips and shook his head at the magma flow of ink and blood. "We're gonna have to redo this soon."

Shane slapped his hands away and said, "My shot." He metronomed his forearm looking down the length of the table with one open eye. Tongue between his teeth split down the middle like a snake, the left end curling up into the wiry hairs growing over his lip.

Cups stacked/table folded/us on the couch. Shane held up a finger and spit blood into an empty beer bottle and smiled. Charlie peered at his cousin's gums and clapped his hands. "Evil, man. Ugly shit."

The next morning Shane was gone. Charlie walked into the living room looking like hell and poured us each a glass of cranberry juice and vodka. We drank it and sat out on his porch. The weather was turning and I didn't have a jacket. Charlie went inside and came out with a hoodie and gave it to me. We watched the folks riding by on bicycles and walking past swinging their arms up to the sky. Men and women without teeth talking to themselves or singing loudly.

A deep low cloud came in and soon it was snowing a bit.

Charlie cursed and got a blue tarp out of his garage and covered the car parts and the frame and weighed it down with cinderblocks.

I set the empty cup down and got a beer from inside and sat back down.

We each tensed against a sudden wind.

I said, "So what's going on with your cousin?"

Charlie arranged the cigarette butts on his porch with his toe. "He's a little off."

"I gathered."

"He does his own thing, I guess."

"And what's that?"

"I'm not sure."

"He grew up here?"

"He moved around."

"Seems like a character."

"Yeah, well," Charlie stood up to get a beer. "He's family."

SLEDDING

We went to Walmart and bought sleds and drove out to the only hill in town. The college stadium was pocked with kids and others like us and we slid down the hill and laughed. We texted friends and soon we had a whole group of us out there.

The whole flat of the land was white and I was freezing in my hoodie but I remember that as the first time I was able to take my mind off things. In my spare time, high or not, I'd been checking my phone and I'd go to her Facebook page and look to see who was liking her status updates. I'd convinced myself that there was a way to tell whether the likes were casual or something else. Most of them came from the man or a few others who I didn't know but they were there and I investigated them thoroughly. I checked their profiles and felt my heart hurt but also I had this odd thing like being stuck in the lobby of a movie theater.

I was living in a present that the past hadn't caught up to yet. I didn't think of anything but that there was this situation and that I had nothing.

But that day when it snowed in October I forgot all about it for a second and all I could think of was how the bulbs on the scoreboard looked so dim and the goal posts stretched up and caught snowflakes in the upturned paint. I watched all my friends slide down the hill, some of them scared and others without any hands at all.

Charlie went down one of those last times and hit a strange bump and flew up in the air and flipped end over end.

When he reached the bottom, he stood up and pumped both his fists in the air.

HOOKUP

Bill's was mostly empty that night but for us and the drunks and two good-looking women sitting at the bar.

The snow had kept on throughout the day and everyone was wrapped up until the night went on.

Eventually the two of us drank enough that we went up to these women and talked. I can't remember what we said but I know myself enough to know that as bad as I am in the long run, I'm just as good in the short. We bought them drinks and on it went and I could see that the one with the tattoos up her arm was looking at me in that way and so we went out into the snow to smoke cigarettes and work on keeping our balance.

Even now, if I smell this woman's perfume somewhere in a room I can pick it out and I get quiet for a long time.

I knew her name, I can say that much.

We fucked in the car and she rode me for about thirty seconds before she got hers and quit. She pulled up her pants in the passenger seat and I kind of looked at my dick and she said, "Well I'm not gonna fucking blow you. You figure it out," and got out of the car and went inside.

I sat there with my pants down and thought to myself, *All right. This is your life now.*

In the car on the way home, Charlie trying not to skid, he asked me for details. When I told him, he said, "She manned you."

"I guess so."

"You got bitched."

"I did indeed."

"So you never got it done?"

"No."

He turned a corner and nearly ran us into a ditch. "Well don't fucking jack off on my couch."

YOU LOOK LIKE AN ASSHOLE

A few days later, Charlie had a big party at his house. He'd ordered a bunch of speed from the internet and everyone there was warm and rolling. Everyone moved between the rooms and said things to each other and I picked out women to talk to but most of them politely found themselves elsewhere.

A few GIs showed up. One of them, Raul, had cocaine and he put a bit of it on the fat of his hand between his thumb and forefinger and I inhaled it.

Raul said, "I saw him die right there. He was looking up and then his eyes went out and he just looked like a dummy. There's a waxy thing to death. I cried like a bitch. I was covered in all of his blood."

His buddy was a wiry fellow who took to annoying anyone he could. This Asian girl showed up and he called her Toyota, Suzuki, Honda.

Raul moved on somewhere else and I ended up next to his friend. He told me I looked like I was bummed and I told him he looked like an asshole and he said, "You're an asshole," so I hit him as hard as I could. He went down and I picked him up by the shirt and hit him over and over. The party quit and everyone surrounded me and him and I got the door open and he had his foot jammed under it like we might let him back in if only he pushed hard enough. He got a good one in and my right eye went shut. We hit him back and finally Charlie came up over me and put out a cigarette on his face and he fell into the snow. He stalked around until Raul peeked his head out and told him to call a cab.

BILLS

At a certain point, days later, Charlie woke me up and handed me a cup of cranberry juice and vodka and sat across from me and asked me what I was planning to do.

I told him I didn't know.

He told me that they were fixing to shut his water off, and that I better figure out what I planned on doing real soon.

I looked around. I picked up applications. I filled them out on paper or in those little kiosk things.

Right around the college campus, there was this restaurant that was just opening up. I saw the 'help wanted' sign and walked in and filled out an application. They pointed me to a table and told me to talk to the owner.

He sat at a table at the far end of the restaurant. Chair pushed out. Big belly heaving under a Looney Tunes t-shirt. Grease stains and barbecue sauce on it.

The owner shook my hand. "What the fuck happened to your face?"

"I tripped and fell on a railing."

He blinked slowly. "What did you do before this?"

"I traveled."

"I mean, job-wise. I'm looking at this application," he picked up the sheet of paper in front of him, "and I don't see any prior work experience."

"I worked at an Arby's when I got out of college."

"You went to college?"

"Yep. Just up the road at Pierce."

"No shit. Graduate?"

I shook my head.

"Be glad you got out. My sons racked up some bills."

"I don't like bills."

"Me neither." The owner sighed. "Listen, your face is fucking weird. Looks like someone knocked the hell out of you. I need a dish guy, but your face is too weird."

I sat there with my hands in my lap.

"You can go now," the owner said.

THE SCAR ON MY LEG

I went out to dinner with my mother. We met at a Chili's. I brought her a plastic bag full of Reese's peanut butter cups. She looked in the bag and her face lit up and that made me happy.

She told me about her work, about how the kids were driving her crazy, about trying to teach them multiplication, about how the mothers came in for conferences still tweaking. We talked about my father and how he was good for nothing. Any time I thought of my father I became deeply afraid.

My mother ordered a daiquiri and she started talking a lot and I'd never seen her drink before.

I asked how my step-father was and Mom said, "He fishes a lot."

We talked about the past.

Mom said, "I remember you and your little brother, you shared a room. You'd set up laundry baskets between the two beds and you'd jump on them and pretend the floor was hot lava. Do you remember that?"

I said, "Yes."

She said, "I remember I told you not to do that. I told you that it was dangerous. But you didn't listen. And one day, you jumped on a laundry basket and you went right through it. And the laundry basket got sharp and cut you."

"Pretty deep. I still have the scar on my leg."

"You're kidding! It didn't go away?"

I said, "No."

We ate some food.

I told her, "I remember you cleaning up the cut in the bathroom, and I was crying, and you said, 'You never listen.'"

She laughed. "That's what I said."

After the meal, she started eating the candy I'd brought her. That made me happy again.

JUGGALO PARTY

Shane had just rolled back into town. Charlie fixed us parachutes. We ate them and drank and dipped to a party.

The Juggalos cracked their beers and freestyled in a circle. Charlie waved his hands about, big hatchet man necklace bouncing against his wife beater. He rapped about stabbing women and raping their corpses over ICP rapping about stabbing women and raping their corpses. The Juggalos put their fists to their mouths and snapped their fingers.

The apartment was small. A tiny Chihuahua weaved between their legs. It jumped in my lap and I picked it up and held it over my head. Shane had shown up earlier that day, and he sat next to me and wiggled his fingers at the dog.

The freestyle circle dispersed. Bass still thumping.

Charlie poured shots of 151 and handed one to his cousin. Shane took the shot and growled. Charlie shouted to the mass of Twiztid shirts and baggy jeans and labret piercings and soul patches, "My nigga failed a job interview today."

The Juggalos golf clapped. I bowed.

"You're my blood," he said and punched me in the shoulder.

Shane clasped his hands in his lap and looked off to the side.

A short, heavyset kid placed a small baggie on the foldout dinner table. Charlie opened it and poured a bit onto the vinyl. "You can see the crystals."

We got high and Charlie told stories to the group.

"I remember when Shane went to jail, like sixteen or something. He was running around outside of Walmart just smashing niggas and taking their bags. Run up behind them and pop, knock their ass out. Just tossed that shit into the trash, man."

Shane sat quietly.

The heavyset kid laughed. "Word."

"There was the time he tried to set his moms on fire."

Shane flinched.

The kid said, "Like, the house?"

"Nah. Like, his actual moms. Just came in the house with some lighter fluid. It was the wildest shit I'd ever seen."

The kid held out a fist. Shane slowly tapped it.

I put the Chihuahua down.

"Or the time with that girl. That was the most brutal shit I'd seen since--"

Shane addressed the heavyset kid. "Studio?"

The Juggalo's eyes lit up. "Yep."

"Let's look at that."

The kid brought him into his room. Jack Skellington curtains and pumpkin bedsheets and a rail thin girl staring at the ceiling holding her chest. He leaned over her. "You alright, baby?"

She smiled. "I'm higher than fuck."

He opened his closet. Cut up egg cartons lined the walls. A mic hung from the ceiling with a sock over it. "This is where I write my masterpieces." Turned on his PC. Brought up some beats. "Let's drop something." Out in the living room, the Juggalos howled. A big girl lifted her shirt up.

Charlie cut out a few more lines. Shane grimaced and grinded his teeth. "I've got shit to do."

His cousin glared at him. "'Shit to do.' Jesus. Put it in your fucking face."

"Charlie."

"Put it in your fucking face."

Shane railed the line.

I didn't need convincing.

The beat came on, lots of snare rolls and bass and organ keys.

The Juggalo said, "Grimy shit."

"Ugly."

"You got something for me?"

Charlie cocked his thumb at Shane. "The homie has bars for days."

I peeked out of the room. A few kids wrapped themselves in Christmas lights and turned on a Kurosawa film. One of them just kept talking, going on about what a master this dude was, look at this shot, that shot, perfectly framed. No one else paid him any mind. Shane said, "That looks like fun."

Charlie said, "Drop some science."

"I don't know."

"Drop knowledge. You're a clumsy librarian."

"I might. I don't know."

"Either do or don't. Weigh your pros and cons. Do it."

Shane tapped his head. "There is no simple math in this dark thing."

The Juggalo let the beat ride out.

Shane thrashed wildly. The Juggalo tagged him twice in his eye. He stumbled back. The heavyset kid moved in. Got him twice more on the chin. Shane landed on his ass in the dirt and the group cheered. Charlie stepped in. "He's done. Enough."

Shane scrambled to his feet. He stalked around the back of his house and came back carrying a giant branch. The bony ends of it scraping against the streetlights.

The Juggalos roared. Charlie held out his hand. "What are you gonna do with that?"

Something left from behind Shane's dilated eyes. He suddenly looked confused. "I'm gonna kill him with this branch."

Charlie picked the tree limb from his cousin's grip. "Go home."

Shane hesitated.

I wrapped my arm around his shoulder. "Come on," I said.

We stumbled down the street.

Charlie turned to the Juggalos. "Normally I'd say come on home with us and smoke something. But when he gets like this…"

Shane howled and I wrapped him up in my arms and carried him.

Charlie shrugged. “I better get on.”

PIRATE SHIP

The next morning I woke up and Shane looked over at me from where he sat and said, "I'm hungry."

We walked to the Corner Store and waved hello the man behind the counter. Shane poured himself a slushie and bought some chips and talked to the clerk a bit and we went out front and sat on a picnic table off to the side and he ate his chips. Watched passersby slip on the ice.

A man in a leather jacket came out of the dark and sat between us. He had a pirate ship tattooed across his face.

He pointed at the tattoo under Shane's eye. "What's this dagger mean?"

"Nothing."

He pointed at the "580" across Shane's chin. "What's this mean?"

"It's the area code."

"Where am I?"

Shane told him.

"Do you have a videogame system?"

"Yeah."

The man rummaged through his bags. Pulled out a loaf of white bread. "I got this bread. Can I come over and play?"

Shane motioned with the bag of chips. "No."

The man was quiet for a bit. "What's these teardrops mean?"

"Means I'm super sad."

"What's this on your neck?"

"It's a Buddha."

"It's a Buddha!" the man yelled. He pointed at the giant tattoo on his face. "You know what this pirate ship means?"

"What?"

The man in the leather jacket hopped up and put his hands on his knees and leaned into Shane's face. "It means I'm a motherfucking PIRATE."

After that the man sat down, put some sunglasses on, ate his bread, and said not one more word to Shane Tilden. He got up and left.

The snow picked up again.

The clerk came out and lit a cigarette. Offered the pack to Shane.

"No, thanks. I only smoke when I drink."

The clerk nodded. "Me, too."

Cars hissed past on the wet road. I took a cigarette.

The clerk said, "You attract them."

"I seem to."

"All that shit on your face."

"Yeah."

We smoked and sat and after a time we went back to Charlie's. Shane gathered his things and left without saying a word.

GO BE NORMAL

I signed up for an online dating site. I spent a lot of time picking the right profile picture.

I couldn't figure what to write in the "About Me" section.

Charlie saw me on the computer and came up and looked over my shoulder.

"OkCupid."

"Yeah."

He took a sip of beer. "They make those for queers, too, you know."

"Shut up."

"You have a kind of sad need for pussy, don't you?"

"I just like it."

"I don't know if that's true."

"I'm not gay."

"That's not what I'm saying."

I turned back to the computer. "I got a message already."

"Have fun fucking weird internet people. I'm gonna go be normal and not get laid until I see something I actually like."

I waited fifteen minutes before I responded to this message. The woman's name was Hanna.

IF I'D MET YOU WHEN I WAS YOUNG, I WOULD HAVE KILLED YOU

That Sunday, Charlie told me we needed to go to church.

I told him I'd pass. He told me they paid $50 just to show up.

I said, "Okay."

The preacher paced at the podium. He raised his arm above his head. "If I'd met you when I was young, I would have killed you."

Dropped his hand on "killed."

The church was cramped. Christmas tree in the corner. Someone coughed.

The preacher smiled. One gold tooth. "If I'd met you when I was young, I would have killed you."

Someone said, "I don't blame you."

He paced faster. Windpants swishing. Despite the cold in the room, he began to sweat. That mantra, repeated as he ran his fingers through wet curly hair: "If I'd met you when I was young, I would have killed you."

Over and over. The room churning a bit. Behind us, someone spoke in tongues.

The congregation said it with him, everyone shouting "killed" with the holy man, his hand chopping the air.

He stopped and so did the crowd.

Took a breath. "My friend Harold was bad. He was bad. If Harold and I met you, back when we were young, we would have killed you."

Leaned on the podium. "Harold had a stomach, he could never keep it down. Anything he ate was gonna tear him up. Changed with the seasons. In the summer he couldn't eat hardly anything without getting sick. In the winter, when it got cold like it is, he could eat everything. Never seen someone eat as much. But just in the winter. Didn't eat more than a sandwich in the summer. He drank a lot of coffee. On top of everything else. His favorite mug had a snake on it. He liked robots and we were roommates and he had to be home to watch his TV with the lasers and I liked them okay, too. I sometimes called him Terminator because he was so tall. In the summer he'd hold his stomach and watch robots. We didn't go out because it was only a matter of time before someone said something. You know how it is. I know you know how it is."

The congregation nodded. Men with small eyes. Women in surplus jackets.

"When we were younger, we killed a man just down the road from here. In the bar talking about his new shoes. Got drunk and we followed him out there and took what was in his wallet, but Harold hit him too hard. We killed people who deserved it and we'd watch robots and wonder on it."

The man behind me amped up the tongues.

The preacher pointed. "That sound, we would have killed you."

The man behind me scaled back the tongues.

"I ate dinner at Harold's house as a child. His father was a good man and his mother was good, too. He had brothers and sisters that had children. He couldn't be that, though. Neither of us could. We were in and out of jail but when we were both out, we were together. I loved Harold. After a time we grew up. I kept a steady job and he did, too. We met women and we moved on and we calmed down. We became men. I had a son. He's a grown man now himself. Harold had a daughter and we'd joke about them getting married but they never did. He once asked me over the phone if I thought it was wrong, how we were, and I said of course it was. No way you could figure it to not be wrong. We were heathens. Godless heathens."

Someone said, "Praise Jesus."

The preacher pushed off the pulpit and put his hands in his pockets. "His guts were gonna take him. Never went to the doctor. At first he couldn't because of money but after a while you just don't think about it. I wonder would it have gotten him. I wonder would he have been watching his stories. I don't know. When he came to my house we went fishing down by the pond and got into an argument about god knows what and god knows we argued all the time, all our lives. But I hadn't seen him in a while and it was the dry heat of summer and that stomach was killing him and the tones of his voice sounded wrong to me and so I hit him. He fell back and landed wrong and he was gone, just like that. I miss him."

The congregation didn't move but for the few folks now recording the sermon on their cell phones.

He scratched the corner of his mouth.

"If I'd met you when I was young, I would have killed you. But then I got old, and I killed Harold."

The preacher closed his eyes and held up a hand. He said, "Let us pray."

We collected our checks from a disinterested secretary and stepped out into the ice and the cold.

Charlie said, "I liked the thing he did with his hand."

"The—" I made a chopping motion.

"Yeah."

"I fucking hate going to church."

"Next time we'll just donate plasma."

IDEAS

Charlie and I went to the Corner Store. He picked out a thirty-pack of Keystone and took it up to the counter.

The clerk said, "You got your ID?"

Charlie nodded and took out his wallet and showed him.

The clerk rang up the beer. He said, "You got any weed?"

Charlie shook his head and paid for the Keystone and left.

YOU KNOW WHAT THEY SAY

I've never been good face-to-face, never been quick on it. There's a term, something about the spirit of the staircase, that thing you might have said, but now there's a delay and we all live on those stairs, waiting for our shoe to drop.

When I met Hanna at the Cellar Bar we were quiet around each other, though we'd written to each other a lot. Then the beer came and we talked and we learned what was real and what was not.

She was in a blue knit cap and a t-shirt.

"Aren't you cold?"

"It's cold out there. But not in here."

She took a paper bag out of her purse and rolled an apple out of it onto the table and started eating it.

"You know what they say," I said.

"Apples are delicious," she said.

I laughed. "I'm not sure that's what they say."

"That's what I say."

"You know what they say: it's really fucking cold outside."

"You know what they say: it's not so cold in here."

A table of old women were celebrating their friend's birthday party. They cheered and sipped margaritas.

"They're into it," Hanna said.

"Having a time," I said.

"I can't get that way anymore."

"Why's that?"

She kind of focused on the space behind my head. "I got too drunk a year ago and threatened to rip my sister's cunt out with barb wire."

At that point, most sensible men might go in a different direction. But at that point, I just needed someone to be close to me. I needed to breathe in the smell of her hair and hold on to her and wake up next to her and brush my teeth with her there in the next room. I felt all of these things and I don't know why because I didn't know this person just the same as I didn't know any of the people I spent my time around. I felt like I'd died and someone new was in my place. I was still coming down off the relationship with my wife and I was thirsty.

I told her about what had happened between my wife and me. It was a truncated version, but I found myself filling in the blank spaces until it became less about the give and take, less about what had happened, and more about how those things had affected me, the way they'd changed me, the way they left me with an emptiness.

It was all true, but I didn't tell it to feel better. I told her that because I knew, somehow, that a woman who might threaten to rip out her sister's privates wouldn't be able to not fuck a man on his way down.

She put her hand over mine and her eyes glazed over.

The old women roared. The birthday girl had unwrapped a giant dildo.

"That's the scariest thing I've ever seen."

"Yeah. They're so into it."

"No, I mean the size of that thing. Jesus."

"Right."

When I dropped her off, I'd just put the car in park and turned the music down when I looked over and saw that she was crying.

Her face was red and puffy.

She reached for my belt.

I pushed her hand away.

She looked at me and said, "Please."

I said, "I think I'll be all right."

She said, "You think I'm ugly."

I said, "That's not it. I think you're pretty. I just don't want to."

Hanna pushed my hands away and undid the belt. She was full-on sobbing now, really getting into it. She took my dick out and it was half-hard.

All teeth.

I braced my hands on the passenger-side headrest and the roof.

Closed my eyes and tried to focus on the warmth and the wetness of it. But the teeth cut into me and eventually I cried out and she quit and sobbed heavily and threw the door open and ran back into her house.

I deleted my account on the dating site later that night.

NOT HUNTING

I told Charlie about what happened the next morning. He was under the Mustang.

"You got bitched again," he said.

"I guess I did."

"You'd better watch out. Next time she's gonna fuck your ass."

"Shut up."

"You take a shower with your clothes on?"

"I took a shower. But I took my clothes off."

"Did you cry?"

"Shut up."

"Man, I'm your friend. But since you came here, you've been just…I don't know."

"What?"

"Different."

"Well, fuck yeah I'm different."

He rolled out from under the car and pointed a socket wrench at me. "I know that shit is fucked up for you right now. But you've gotta get it together. I'm your friend. You need to listen to me. You're like a thirsty woman but it's worse because you're supposed to be a dude. You're different. If you're gonna be different, at least be a man about it."

We were quiet for a long time. Wind chimes down the street.

We walked inside and didn't talk to each other.

The pilot light on the fridge kicked on.

Finally, I said, "All right. You're right."

"Of course I'm right. So here's what we're gonna do. We're gonna go out to the Last Call tonight, and you're gonna hang out and drink some beer and we're gonna talk about our dicks and comment on the size of all the titties we see. But you're not gonna pursue like some sad little queer."

"Okay. I'm down."

"And you need to get a fucking job or something, man. One, you need to occupy your time. Two," he stabbed his finger at a stack of bills.

"I've been on the job hunt."

"You're like a dog looking out the window at squirrels."

"I've been trying."

"Not hunting, is all I'm saying."

"I don't know what I'm trying to do."

Charlie loaded the bowl. "Probably you should smoke some weed about it."

VESTMENTS

We ate a couple rolls each and met up with Shane at Last Call. Machine gun music in the jukebox. Rednecks and metal kids and women in glitter.

Charlie pointed at a woman in a halter top. "Big titties," he said.

"Big titties," we echoed.

Shane's pupils were huge. He said, "Picture me like this. Picture me reaching enlightenment."

"Like, dying?" Charlie bounced in place in his chair.

"Nah, like, picture me as this old ass monk. In all the vestments."

"The fuck is a 'vestment?'"

"Like a robe and I'm bald and shit."

We pictured it. A woman in short-shorts walked by. Charlie said, "Shelf booty."

"Shelf booty," we echoed.

"I guarantee you that I could meet the Buddha. He could come down and talk to me and there'd be gold light and shit and me and him would go out into a garden and I'd feel at peace with fucking everything.

I guarantee you this: even if that was the case, if a hoodrat nigga like you came to me with some of this shit, I would ingest it post haste and run slamdancing down the halls of my monastery."

Charlie said, "I have no idea what the fuck you just said. But I am higher than a motherfucker."

"Me too," Shane said. "Me too."

A woman in a sweater and mom jeans leaned over the bar. We all tilted our heads.

Charlie took a sip of beer. "I'd hit it."

"I'd hit it," we echoed.

MALKUTH

We invited everyone we knew to the crib that night and it was off the fucking chain in that motherfucker I am telling you right now. Shane decided that his gums needed a touch up and everyone stood around geeking and some of them had the red Solo cups with the Sprite and shit in them and they were seeing the people in the shadows worming their way through the spackle in the ceiling. That sound, that sound was something else, that sound makes me gag to this day, the needle hitting bare pink gum and flooding over. I wonder how much fucking ink he swallowed in those sessions, I wonder how toxic it was, and I wonder if that was why he was the way he was. A kid with long hair and an acoustic guitar sat on the arm of the couch and played songs for the girls until his gun slipped from the back of his jeans and he retrieved it and took one of the girls back to the room. A big son of a bitch that I'd never seen before talked shit in the kitchen and stood on his head and poured beer into his face and everyone laughed and carried on. Kenny was there, too, fucking Kenny. We fucked with that kid throughout high school, we were fucking merciless, we'd be out on the soccer field that no one used for soccer by the turnaround where the kid with the beamer took his girlfriends and we'd put Kenny in a shopping cart because Kenny didn't have a family that cared about him, he had a dad and his dad was a real piece of shit but Kenny was small and sad and so we pushed him in this shopping cart right into an open port-a-john that tipped over and spilled everywhere and he was covered in it and we fucking laughed. That night we were digging into the speed and beer, I love the way a half-empty box of Coors feels when you reach into it when it's sitting there on the floor and you can feel the cold air still in it like whatever the opposite of a tomb is, and then it's even colder when you get the beer itself. But that night the boy with the long hair and the gun took the girl out of the room and the girl he was with discovered that while they were busy Kenny stole the girl's purse and so Shane decided we needed to do something about this. He called up Kenny's friend Damon who gave him up right away, told us he'd be at this hotel room holed up. We went into Charlie's room and he opened his drawer and lifted up the snake coil of fake ass chains and yelled, "I got chains on chains nigga!" and then beneath those was a pile of bandanas, a hodgepodge, ICP and Peanuts and a blue paisley one and one from Chili's and one from Disney World. It's at that point that Shane took me aside to the guest room and he told me that he had a spell that would protect me and I was so gone there was three of him. He drew a pentagram on the wall and did a chant and I only remember the word

"Malkuth" and then he slapped me on the shoulder and said, "heathens" and suddenly I saw the pentagram on the wall and it was on fire but it gave no heat. I said, "heathens" and I felt the last little bit of who I was fall asleep. And five of us, Shane and Charlie and the new me and the acoustic man and the big son of a bitch, we piled into the big boy's truck and off we headed. We slapped on the bandanas and banged on the hotel door but he wouldn't answer and we had a bat and the door opened quick and the purse dropped out and we grabbed it and piled back in the truck and tore off. We got the girl her purse back but it was missing the wallet and the phone. Shane and I ran out into the field out there and we didn't have any shirts and we shouted "heathens" and the moon wasn't even full that night.

MORNING AGAIN

Later that night when it was morning again I got a text message from my wife. My eyes were shaking so hard my temples hurt but I pursed my lips and stared.

It said, "I hope you are doing well. I miss you. I worry about you. Do you remember when we were younger and I was leaving? We stood by the van until it got so late. I just want you to know that you'll always be my soulmate. I love you."

I didn't know what to make of that.

I put my phone under the bed and tried to sleep.

The room turned blue with the dawn.

HARD IN THE PAINT

When I woke up, Shane was exercising in front of the TV. One of those Wii fitness games. He held the controllers at his side and pretended to jump rope.

I still had my Peanuts bandana tied around my face.

Charlie was in the kitchen cooking breakfast.

The game dinged and told Shane he did a good job.

Charlie came out of the kitchen with a skillet and picked up a plate off the end table and licked it clean. He slid the eggs from the skillet onto the plate and handed them to Shane.

The tattooed man sat down across from me and held out the plate. "Eggs?"

I thought I might throw up. I shook my head.

"Gotta have some protein."

From the kitchen: "I've got some protein for you in my nuts."

Shane frowned. "Don't be gross." He looked at me and chewed slowly. Finally: "You don't do this much, do you?"

"What?"

"Go hard in the paint. We go hard in the paint. You

don't go very hard in the paint, do you?"

"Recently, yeah. But no, I guess not."

"The thing about going hard in the paint--"

From the kitchen: "Quit fucking saying that."

"You need to hydrate."

Charlie brought some water. "He's right. Drink."

I drank it.

Shane said, "Eat an egg."

"No thanks."

"One egg."

"I'll fucking puke."

To Charlie: "Hey, do you still have that whey stuff?"

From the kitchen: "Yeah."

"Mix this man a smoothie."

Charlie brought me a glass of water mixed with whey powder. Chunks floating in it. I closed my eyes and drank the whole thing and focused on not gagging.

Shane finished his eggs and set the plate down. He leaned forward and looked at me.

I said, "What?"

"The cops would have come by now, if they were going to at all."

I felt sick again.

"You don't have to worry. Why would they call? They stole from us."

The two of us sat in silence for a long time. Charlie in the kitchen. Shane just staring at me.

"Jesus Christ. What?"

"I'm only just learning this, so I'm having trouble figuring it out."

"Figuring what out?"

"Your aura."

From the kitchen: "Your aura is gay."

"Don't be rude."

"You have the aura of a gay man."

"I'm serious. I can't tell if you're a dark red. If you're a dark red, that means you're a sexual being."

Charlie started doing the dishes. Over the sound of the faucet: "Please stop hitting on my friend."

"How did you meet my cousin?"

I felt uncomfortable. He didn't blink.

"From school," I said. "We've known each other since school."

"I've never seen you here."

Over the sound of the faucet: "He's been married and shit."

"Is he a deeply sexual person?"

A pause. "He's a dude."

Shane made a noise and leaned back in his chair. "It might be more of a clouded red. That means you're a deeply angry person. Like, anger that you almost can't control."

Charlie said, "Not bad," and I said "That's true."

"But…there's also a little bit of dark blue. Navy blue. You don't know what the future holds. You want to control the present moment. You've lost that control. It's like a blue going into a red, like a…"

Charlie: "Like a Fruit Roll-Up."

Shane snapped his fingers. "Exactly! Like a fucking Fruit Roll-Up."

I said, "Are you a fortune teller? Is that what you do?"

Shook his head. "I don't know the future. If I knew the future, I would already be living in it. What do you do?"

"Nothing, now."

"What did you do?"

"I worked in the mall."

He nodded.

I said, "What color is Charlie's aura?"

Shane said, "Charlie's aura is pink."

Charlie shut the faucet off. "You're gay."

"He's gifted. But it can grow dark. Deceitful."

"What's your aura?"

"I'm indigo. I can see the other worlds."

"Like the future, then."

"No, just other worlds. Sometimes they're ahead of us, sometimes they're behind. Like, for example. Me and a buddy had a trunk full of hydro and we were coming in from California. I had this vision. Came to me clear. It was Jehovah's Witnesses coming to my door. I brought them in and gave them tea. So I tell my buddy, we have to dress like Jehovah's Witnesses. He thought I was nuts. But we did, and on the way here, it was really snowy, icy, and we drove our car into a ditch. The cops came by and saw us there and saw that we were godly, and they helped us out of the ditch. Never searched the car."

"That sounds like telling the future to me."

"If I knew the future I'd know that we would crash and if I knew that I'd already be crashing. It's not knowing the future. It's reading the messages."

Charlie sat down and picked up a bong and packed the bowl. "Don't listen to him."

"You were married."

I got quiet.

"Now you're not?"

"I'm still married."

Shane reached for the bong. Charlie gave it to him, still holding the smoke in his lungs. "You know what you're telling me?"

My brain wasn't moving quickly enough. I just shrugged.

Shane inhaled. Let it out. "You should go back to your wife and apologize for whatever you've done."

"I didn't--"

"That's what I'm saying. That's what you *should* do."

The room was quiet. The videogame asked us if we were ready to jog in place.

"I don't know you," I said.

"That's true," he passed me the bong. "But, I think I know you. I know what you should do. But you're not there yet. And besides. You're a fucking heathen now. You don't work?"

"No."

Shane got up and came back with a duffle bag. I coughed out the smoke. He unzipped the bag and brought out a giant mason jar full of weed on the coffee table. A Ziploc fat with sheets of acid. Another pregnant with ecstasy.

"This is what I do."

I looked at the table, then back to him.

"Do you want to sell some drugs?"

I glanced over at Charlie. Engrossed in his phone. Back to Shane. "Sure," I said.

He smiled at me. "How do my gums look?"

"Ugly, man. Evil shit."

GIFT CARD

We bought white t-shirts from Walmart and cut them with a pocket knife and put them on. We bought fake blood from Party America and poured it over our heads.

Shane put the weed and the pills and the sheets in a backpack and cut open a blue bag of MDMC and dumped it onto a cutting board. He emptied Niacin pills in the sink, the tiny beads clinking in the tin. Scooped the white powder into the capsules and capped them off and licked his fingers. He tore off little strips of paper towels and sprinkled the speed onto them and balled them up and we parachuted them. I downed mine with a beer and nearly gagged.

He gave me ten pills and Charlie twenty. We put them in our pockets.

"Shit hasn't been tested yet, it's still an RC. So they're not technically illegal. But when we put them in the pills like that, it's kind of illegal." He paused. "It's a gray area. But it's less dangerous than all that shit," pointing at the backpack, "so I'll start you off with a low risk."

The speed took hold and I listened and I grit my teeth.

"They get one for twenty or they can get two for thirty."

"What about three?"

"Three is fifty."

"Okay."

"Anything over one, the last is half. No more than that."

Shane was DJing at the Last Call. He set up his mixers in the booth and arranged the songs he was going to play. I stood in there with Charlie and looked out at the kids arriving, all of them in zombie makeup and ripped shirts.

Shane said, "You look nervous as a chinaman in a dick-measuring contest."

I said, "I'm not nervous."

He said, "Low risk. Don't worry."

I said, "I'm not."

When we got back to Charlie's, we dumped our earnings on the small pool table in the corner. We picked through the money and divvied it up.

Shane held up a Walmart gift card. "Fuck is this?"

I told him, "It's got $25 on it."

"Does it?"

"I think so."

He handed it to me. "Cash, man. Cash."

SLOWLY SLIPPING

I met my mother at Chili's the next day and after all the small talk she asked me what was going on with me and my wife.

I told her that she said I was an angry person. I told her about how she started to talk to others. I told her that it was a feeling of slowly slipping. I didn't really know what else to say. She cried and told me that she couldn't stand to see me that sad.

We finished our food and I told her, "I brought you a present."

I handed her the Walmart gift card and hoped there was actually money on it.

II

IMAGINATION

Shane and I walked from Charlie's house to the bookstore next to the Walmart. Along the side of the store a man wearing leggings and a long shirt hopped over a small ditch run through with a trickle of brackish water. He saw us walking in and waved us over.

"Watch this shit."

He jumped over the ditch.

We didn't say anything.

"Now check this shit out."

He jumped back over it.

"That's the castle and I'm jumping over the moat."

He wasn't wearing any shoes.

We went inside. I browsed the shelves and picked out a few books and thumbed through them and went and sat in one of the chairs set up for customers. Shane sat next to me and tore the plastic off a porn magazine.

I flipped through my book and glanced over at him. "You do realize there's this thing called the internet, yeah?"

He licked his thumb and turned a page. "I'm old school."

"Old school."

He tapped his head. "Can't let the mind waste away. Gotta use the old imagination."

I saw a picture of a woman having sex with a bedpost. "Imagination."

"Mm-hmm."

I read the first chapter of the book. Shane chuckled next to me.

I got up and got some coffee. Sat back down. "So where did you get off to last night?"

"Had a big delivery to make."

"Yeah?"

"Yep. House out in Turtle Creek."

"Hood shit?"

"Not really. High school hey-bitches."

I placed the book in my lap. "High school?"

"Yeah, like fifteen, sixteen. Something."

"Oh."

"In the trap, though."

"I see."

"Yep. Got like three hundo and a phone full of titty pics. Overall I'd say that's a win." He plopped the magazine down on the endtable between us. "What's that shit?"

I showed him the book I was reading.

"That seems nice. You should buy that and let me read it. I've been having trouble sleeping."

He stuck his tongue out at me. Split like a snake's.

I said, "Mr. Imagination over here."

Shane thumbed through the pictures in his phone. "Keeps me out of prison."

UZI UP ON INSTAGRAM

Got a text from a number I'd never seen. I told them to meet me at the Cellar. I ordered a Natty Light and leaned against the bar. Few weeks ago they'd done it up for Halloween, rubber rats all along the back bar, skulls with light-up eyes and witches and a mummy in the corner. Taken it all down and replaced it with tinsel and a Christmas tree, but they hadn't taken the time to get the cobwebs down from the cross beams and the chipped ceiling tiles. I plucked a wisp off my beer and balled it up and dropped it over the side of the bar.

Hank Williams on the jukebox. The old white folks roared and howled. The bartender sat on a stool with her legs crossed, engrossed in her phone.

I looked over at the thin man playing the slot machine in the corner.

"You winning?"

The man blinked behind his round glasses. "It's not a money machine."

I took a sip. "I've seen you pump a hundred dollars in that thing."

The thin man pressed the red square. The slots spun on the TV screen. "Twenty maybe."

"Yeah."

"It's my stress relief."

I shrugged.

"You need some stress relief."

"I got this eucalyptus candle."

His face lit up. "Those are good. The three-wick?"

"The three-wick."

The man nodded at me and pressed the button on his slot machine.

My customer pulled the heavy door back and stepped in. I could feel the cold all the way at the back. He weaved around the pool tables and the cowboy hats that turned one eighty to watch him take his seat and hold up a finger to the bartender.

"And I thought it was white outside."

I held out my hand. "Nice to meet you."

He took it and smiled at me. "Richard Beck."

Beck paid for his beer and the bartender brought him a couple quarters back. He spun one of the coins and leaned back. "I feel like I'm about to be lynched."

It had gotten quieter. I told him, "Let's just finish our beers and we can head out to my car."

He nodded.

We sat in silence for a long time. A talent show on the TV. Big girl belting something out. The jukebox quit and the bar was quiet.

Beck said, "She'll never make it."

"Nope."

"America only has five seats in its heart for fat entertainers, and they're taken up by Adele and Precious."

I blew beer out my nose and signaled for another.

"What happened to 'finish the beer?'"

"Oh shit. Sorry."

Beck said, "Two whiskeys."

The bartender handed us two beers. "Just a beer bar."

"No liquor?"

She stared at him. "Well, it's just a beer bar."

I said, "I've seen tons of liquor in this place."

The bartender's eyelids went sharp and she put her hands on her hips.

Beck turned to me. "Bro, please."

I began chugging my beer. Beck followed suit.

As we caught our breath we watched a man in a velvet tie-dye sweatsuit talk to a pool stick. Tipped his tie-dye cap back and rubbed chalk on the stick's end. Still whispering to it.

Beck grabbed my shoulders in mock panic. "Save me from these honkies."

We headed out into the snow and watched our feet.

Beck tapped my shoulder. "Sample."

I gave him one.

He made a face. "Hate dry swallows."

My car was parked in the alley behind the bar. We got in and I turned the car on and blasted the heater. I gave him the pills and he gave me a roll of twenties.

The speed started to take effect. He talked a mile a minute. He asked me if I rapped, and I told him no.

He asked me if I knew anyone who rapped. I said no. He asked me if I had an Instagram.

I said, "I know what it is, but I don't have one yet."

He reached into his pocket and took out his phone. "I'm gonna show you some shit, my friend."

"I don't really have the eye for it."

"Hold up. Hold up. Check this shit out." He held out his phone. "Scroll through."

A picture of an Uzi.

"That's my Uzi."

"You put a picture of an Uzi on Instagram?"

"Hell yeah. I got my boy to set it up. It's like, triple locked or some shit. He knows computers and phones and like, technology. It's all good."

I scrolled. Three men in ski masks. They didn't have shirts on. They were standing in front of a table holding up several pounds of cocaine.

"Real shit."

I scrolled. There was a video of five men beating a man. The man was holding his head and screaming at them to stop. They yelled back that this is what happens when you're a pussy-ass bitch.

"Put that nigga in the hospital. Look at his shoe fly off! His shoe done ran for help."

I scrolled. A woman fellated the cameraman. In the background, on a mattress, a girl lay prone. Several men stood over her. One man crouched behind.

I handed the phone back. "They'll shut down your account for shit like that."

Beck looked at me like I was crazy. "No one's gonna report shit. This is like a documentary."

"It's very raw."

"Straight raw, man. Everything on this earth is straight raw." He glanced down at his phone. The video was still playing. He laughed. "This bitch needs better friends."

DISC GOLF

There was a disc golf course down the road from Charlie's house.

Shane tossed his disc and it went wide and hit a tree. The branches shook and ice sloughed off them to break on the hard snow. We gave him shit and he flipped us off.

"Can't wait for those biscuits," Charlie said.

"The biscuits are the best part," I said.

"I'm not buying either of you biscuits." Shane stepped aside so Charlie could throw.

His disc landed near the goal.

Shane frowned. "Shit."

I geared up for mine. Did a couple practice tosses. I hurled it. It hit the very same tree and landed next to Shane's.

"Maybe we're both buying biscuits," I said.

"We can't both lose."

We hiked down to our discs.

Shane said, "I ran into five-oh last night."

Charlie's eyebrows raised.

"Nothing happened. I was just going to sell. It was like two, two-thirty. When I got there cops were everywhere."

"So you dipped?"

"I asked them what was going on."

I blinked. "You didn't."

"I did."

Charlie said, "You have got to be some kind of retard."

I said, "What was going on?"

Charlie put his hand on Shane's chest. "If you bring that shit to my house, I swear to god."

Shane picked his disc up and brushed the snow off. "No one's bringing anything to your house."

I asked again: "What was going on?"

Shane tossed his disc. It landed wide. "I don't know. Something about a guitar and nunchucks."

BEAST

Charlie's house was packed again.

Same shit.

Shane looking at me, telling me, "I do believe we have gotten silly again."

Me sitting with the two of them, going on about how we could take this even further. The money was good now, sure, but we could take it up a notch. Hire folks to do shit for us. There wasn't a reason not to, I'd say.

Charlie humored me and Shane didn't understand what humor was, same as most people who laugh too much.

He took me aside and told me, "I'll work on it."

A cheer from the garage.

A group of folks I didn't know were out there smoking cigarettes and this big Samoan kid was hitting a punching bag so hard the damn thing went near perpendicular to the wall. He stepped away from it and said, "I'm a beast," and we all told him he was a beast. A tweaker took me aside and started up. His girlfriend was pregnant and he was scared. "I'm looking forward to being a dad, I'm gonna be the best dad ever," he said, "but I don't know." He bit the inside of his cheek and shifted from foot to foot. I tried to focus. He went on about his own father and how he wouldn't do that, and I nodded and paid attention though my mind was thirty places at once.

Most notably my attention was on the girl on the couch.

When the garage party dissipated, Shane went back inside and looked back at me and mouthed the words "next level" and then it was just us and I sat across from her. She had a bunch of holes in her jeans and I told her "I can see your pussy through those rips," and she spread her legs a little wider and she smiled and got up and left.

DAY-TO-DAY

I ignored the texts from my wife.
I ignored the texts from my mother.
I shut down all my social media accounts.
I woke up to the powder and I fell asleep shaking.

POSSUM

The ink had started to take and so Shane's gums turned black.

He handed us each a button of peyote.

The temperature had dropped that night. The snow came down. The three of us huddled in the tornado shelter in Charlie's backyard. We had 40s and a case of beer and a bit of pot. There was a sac of black widow eggs in the far corner and we contemplated leaving, but eventually we convinced each other that black widow babies aren't born under snow.

Shane lit a cigarette and handed one to me. I crushed the menthol ball in the filter. Snow flurries whipped down the concrete steps and we closed the top and breathed in the dirt and the mint smoke.

Shane said, "Last night I was so high I could see around corners. I want to say that I was blackout drunk, too, but I don't think that's right because I can remember things."

The light from the lone bulb hanging cast shadows over his face. His tattoos moved down his forehead, across his cheeks, dripped off his chin.

"Started off at the Dragon."

"The Dragon!" we echoed, and raised our beers.

"I met up with Cassandra there. She was dancing. I made it rain."

"Cassandra," Charlie said. He made his hands into claws and held them out in front of his chest.

"Oh yeah. So I get a private dance and we're talking about this and that. It's almost like a checklist. Boyfriend problems, drug problems, on and on. While she's telling me this, though. She starts choking me."

"Choking, like…your dick?"

"My throat. She's choking me. Fucking strangling me. But I rolled with it. It was kind of nice. I saw stars and passed out and when I came to I felt a lot better about life in general."

The shelter was my ribcage and it was moving.

"I went back to her sister's place. They were gone for the night. She gave me a tuggie in her niece's room. That was weird. Toys everywhere."

"Did you skeet on the toys?"

"I skeeted on her."

Charlie said, "Good man."

"So after that, we went over to her neighbors house and smoked meth in their basement. I gave them a ride to the casino. They were these old-ass Indians. The woman had a face that looked ready to fall off. We went to the casino and they gambled and I gambled a bit too. Lost like fucking two hundo on that shit. But the old Indian chick had this prosthetic leg, and she'd sit at the blackjack table and she'd try to use her leg like a sword. Tried to knight the dealer. When she was at the slots, she'd try to knight the slot machine. The place was mostly empty at this time of night and it was weird quiet. I got on my knee and I let her knight me. Then the stripper hey-bitch and I went to her dealer's house and he fucked her in this room and I just went through all his shit. Got cash, I got a machete."

"I'll trade you for the machete."

"I gave you the railroad knife."

"I'll trade you that for the machete."

"I made that knife. I put care into it."

"But I'll trade you."

I thought of using a machete to hack through thick ferns and at the center of all the trails I met a jaguar.

"I got this, too." Shane reached into his pocket. A Ziploc bag. He took out the sheet of acid and tore it into ten-strips and dropped one each into our respective 40s.

We chugged the malt liquor.

Charlie said, "That's a crazy story, man."

"Yeah."

"I can't believe you got a squeezer from Cassandra."

Outside was like staring into a chasm. The snow had dusted the backyard and underneath it there was a black earth shifting. A possum clung to the chainlink fence. We all took a good look at it but the thing didn't move.

We wondered if it was dead.

We wondered if it was real.

I picked up a stick to poke the thing.

Shane said, "Don't poke the possum."

I walked toward it, holding the stick like a lance. "I'm gonna poke it."

Shane stepped in front of me. "Don't poke the fucking possum."

I put the stick down. "All right. Jesus."

We all kind of stood out there for a moment. Then we went back inside.

We smashed all the potted plants in the house. We lay on the floor and bit into Keystone cans and poured the beer on our faces. We stripped naked and stood in the kitchen. There was a standing inch of beer on the linoleum and there were purple and green layers to it and I dug my toes into it like sand.

Charlie and Shane melted and stepped out of time and space.

Shane yelled, "I've got the big one coming. The big job. The big money."

I went into the guestroom and lay on the floor. My asshole felt very warm. I put my palm between my butt cheeks and looked at it, checking to see if I'd crapped myself.

I shivered and the spackle in the ceiling bled and dipped.

Two aliens appeared before me in the corner. Their heads shaped like windmills.

Purple fog at their feet. They dressed in shirts that hung off one shoulder and I could see their bra straps.

They showed me the weapon of the apocalypse. Three shapes.

I shut my eyes and went to the deepest door in my brain and opened it and touched the darkest ink. They told me if I didn't get away, I would die.

I checked my ass again.

For as long as I was awake, I was convinced that I was shitting on the floor.

DRYWALL

I woke up and stepped out onto the porch. The ice in the trees let light through and skeletons coming up over the tops of the section 8 housing was the most beautiful thing I'd ever seen.

I felt new.

Charlie was leaning into the guts of the Mustang. Hood propped up and buckling with the wind.

When he saw me he stopped what he was doing and turned.

"What's the big thing?"

"What big thing?"

"Shane. What Shane was talking about?"

"I don't know."

"Whatever it is, don't do it."

"Okay."

"I'm serious."

"Okay."

"I'm serious. I love my cousin. But that motherfucker is nuts. Before you met him, he was in prison. Do you know why he was in prison?"

I just wanted to look at the ice on the trees. “No.”

“He came home one day. He had this big pit bull. While he was gone, the pit bull had eaten a chunk out of his drywall. So he dragged the thing out onto his front yard and beat it to death.”

I kicked a rock off the porch. I suddenly realized how cold it was.

Charlie wiped his black hands off on a rag. “Be careful. That’s all I’m saying.”

THAT'S THE WAY

Last Call hosted a fake orgasm contest.

We got drunk and headed over. Shane entered and sat down looking pleased with himself. I tried to picture him murdering a dog. He stuck his split tongue out at me. I could maybe see it. Charlie had been quiet all day. He kept with that vibe at the bar.

Shane said, "I found out this morning that Cassandra's boyfriend has been beating on her."

Charlie said, "She's a stripper. That's part of the job."

Shane said, "I invited the entirety of the Comanche bloods over to his house tonight. Told them it was a big party. Lots of beer."

I couldn't help it. I laughed.

Shane had a way about him.

Some of the contestants were very good. The young girls imitated what they'd seen in porn, which was fine by us. An old woman with big hair and a sparkly Eiffel Tower shirt moaned monotone and said, "That's it. That's the way."

We repeated that throughout the night. "That's the way."

Shane got up and took the mic. Tone Loc's "Wild Thing" faded into the background. He said, "Ah! Awe, shit. Sorry about that."

Everyone went wild.

He sat back down and we killed more beers and he leaned over to me and said, "We're gonna sell hippy crack at the Rage Rave down in Texas."

"Yeah?"

"I got the nitrous from a local. We're gonna go down there and they're gonna give us two grand each."

Charlie looked over at me, his beer poised halfway between the table and his face.

A large woman lay on her back on the stage with her legs in the air and yelled, "Fuck me till I go back in time. Right there. That's dead center. Right on the money!"

I said, "Hell yeah. I'm in."

HIPPY CRACK

Rockville was two gas stations and a post office. Farmland. Tobacco fields out to the horizon. The festival sprung up from the sparse trees. Steel spires and flashing neon lights and girls in belly shirts, their skin painted pink. Boys with no shirts at all. Hyperventilating kids lay prone in the bitch tent, EMTs asking them if it felt strange when they touched their arms. I bought a funnel cake.

I inhaled a balloon before going out to sell. Curiosity. Everything went white and my head rang and then it was gone.

Five dollars for *this*?

Shane inhaled one every fifteen minutes or so. He'd giggle and I'd tell him to focus.

I didn't try to make sense of the appeal. No point. White people are smiling enigmas.

The unwashed masses had lined up through the parking lot, this long snake, and I filled their balloons, took their five or made change, and they'd inhale it right there, some of them stumbling, flaccid Mohawks plastered against their young faces already going tight and lined with abuse.

I saw most of them two, three times. Everybody seemed to sweat under the cool sun. I shed my hoodie early in the day, but once night fell I went back and put it on. Texas weather swinging.

At the end of the day we left the empty canisters in the parking lot and walked to our car. Set the heavy bag of cash in the floor and covered it with our backpacks. We sat down and started the car. We saw the women moving toward the rave, the cutoff shorts and long legs and smooth skin, and I turned the car off.

Thought about it.

We went back through security and into the party.

I bought a beer from a vendor and watched a DJ play a set. Kids in giant glowing fish costumes walked by on stilts. Hippies rode tandem bikes. Women hula hooped and men wore gloves with LED tips, spinning them, the colors flashing. I drank another beer.

We decided to roll.

Three minutes to find a kid with a backpack. Little green X pill down the hatch.

The bass swept over and through me. My chest expanded.

Shane scampered off to the foam machine.

I wandered.

A giant, hairless man stood in a field between two large Tesla coils. He held a metal rod in each hand. Arms outstretched. Webs of current flowing through him. The coils cracked and buzzed. He smiled electric blue.

I popped gooseflesh and felt the music. It rained and I shivered and I was a creature inside of a tree in a bed of mud in a rainforest. The women passed me and I could feel the tightness of their bellies and I could picture their faces twisted and how I could take them in my hands and lay them down.

I went to piss in a port-a-john and my legs shook. Zipped up, sure that I'd wet myself. And then I was sure that the port-a-john had blasted off into space and that if I opened the door I'd fall back to earth. Stayed cooped in there forever, steady breathing, trying to convince myself it would all be okay. Folks banging to get in.

When I finally opened the door, the ground rippled like the ocean and I stumbled through the tangles of bodies and saw young men and women lined along the fence. I joined them and vomited with them and saw the stars swirl in tight whirlpools, the last little bit down the drain forever over and over.

Shane laid his hands on the fence and hurled. He looked at me with eyes as wide as a child's. "There was something wrong with that X."

We stumbled back to the car.

Out my windshield, I saw the music festival disappear and reappear, blinking in and out of existence like a turn signal.

SPIDERS

I dreamt I had a son. I called my mother and told her. I went shopping and the kid was in a stroller. He looked just like me. Then he turned into a tiny blue and red spider and a dog came out of nowhere and ate him, so I shoved my hands down her throat and made her throw him up. I woke up sifting through the pile of vomit, wondering how I was gonna tell my mother that she wasn't a grandma anymore.

HE SAID A CLOUD

We woke up to a cop rapping on our window.

In that moment you take stock of everything you've done with your life.

He told us to move on.

I turned on the car and my head felt heavy and we drove.

He found us at a Love's not fifty miles from the rave. Had to have clocked us instantly: two fuck-ups hunched over taquitos at a Formica booth. He loomed. I recognized him. I grew up with him. Shane must have known. He picked up his phone and hit a button.

"This is all being recorded."

Danny Ames borrowed a chair from a neighboring table and sat down. "My throat hurts. I'm gonna sound bad."

I said, "It goes to a cloud."

"Yeah," Shane still had a taquito in his other hand. "Saved to a cloud."

Men in sandals bought bags of chips and soda.

Women browsed dreamcatchers. Kids pointed up at the animal heads mounted over bottles of motor oil.

Ames laughed. "He said 'a cloud.'"

We looked at each other.

"No, but seriously. That's cool." Ames cleared his throat. "Am I sounding hoarse?"

Shane said, "You sound good."

"Oh, okay. I hate to tell y'all this, but you're gonna have to give me all that shit in your trunk."

For a moment, we just looked at him. At each other. Ames saw it all click and his muscles relaxed.

Shane said, "They're gonna kill us."

Ames shrugged. "Yeah."

We loaded the canisters into the Impala. Ames slammed the trunk and put his keys in his pocket. Anubis on the keychain. He copied our names and addresses from our driver's licenses onto his smartphone.

Shane toed rocks in the asphalt. "So what happens now?"

"I've seen it go both ways."

"Which ways?"

Ames peeked in the bag at the cash. "Imagine the two ways it could go. I've seen both. I won't see it either way."

The Ozarks hid behind a fog. Shane said, "At least beat our asses or some shit."

Danny Ames took a vape pen from his pocket, pressed the button. Cinammon. "We're in the parking lot of a Love's. Beat your own asses."

He got into his car. Shane said, "They're gonna kill us," again.

"Don't care. Make sure you tell Eloise that Danny Ames took her shit. Make sure you're clear about that."

I pointed at his teeth. "Do those come out?"

"What?"

"Your grill. Are the teeth permanent, or can you take them out?"

Danny Ames opened his mouth and pulled out his platinum dentures. Grinned bare gums. "I can take them out whenever," he said.

THE NEAR-MISS

"It's slippery out," Shane said on the drive home. "We could flip the car. We could say that we flipped the car and when the cops showed up they confiscated the money."

I shook my head.

"We could do what we said. We could hit each other."

"I'm not going to hit you. Or get hit."

Shane turned in his seat. Prairie rolling by out the window. "Do you understand how fucked we are?"

I nodded.

"There was a lot of money. That was a *lot* of money."

"I know that."

"We should flip the car. The cops come."

"We're both still a little high. I'm not flipping the car."

"I should have brought a gun."

"You don't have a gun."

"I should have bought a gun."

"You wouldn't have used it."

"I would have shot him."

"You were just as scared as I was."

Shane chewed his thumbnail. "Your aura is different."

I took a deep breath. "Oh yeah?"

"It's yellow but I don't know which yellow. You're either afraid or you've come to some new point in your life."

"I don't know if I came to a new point in my life. I think I remembered a point from before all this. You know the feeling you get when you almost get in an accident? You just barely miss the car coming at you. You know that adrenaline? That's what I've got right now. I feel like I forgot. I feel like I forgot that I'm the guy who gets pulled over for running a red light. I forgot that the universe has this conception of me as someone who does the right thing. Good things. I don't know how I forgot that."

Shane was quiet for a bit. "We're just different."

"I think so."

"I'm the guy who can't ever see his mother. You know she has a restraining order on me?"

"I know."

"We owe a ton of money to people who have made other people disappear for far less."

"We'll figure it out. I'll get a job. We'll pay them back."

"You've still got that adrenaline going?"

"Definitely."

"I wish I could say I understood it. You're the near miss, but I'm the oncoming car."

He reached for the wheel and turned it. I stomped on the brakes and the car spun. It stopped on the side of the road and the engine died.

When I started hitting Shane, I'd only meant to knock some sense into him. Eventually he was yelling stop, and after a few more I put him out.

I fired up the ignition and drove us home.

NEW BOSS

A week later we were sitting in the living room. Charlie cut out lines on the coffee table. None of us spoke. We hadn't said more than a couple words to each other since we got back from Rockville.

Two large men came through the door carrying guns.

Charlie hopped up and said, "I know you're not coming in here on some bullshit."

They pointed the guns at Charlie.

He said, "At least knock."

The big man on the left said, "I'm Turtle, and this is Little John."

Charlie said, "Turtle. John."

Turtle noticed Shane sitting on the recliner. "Shane! Why don't you answer your texts, fool?"

Shane looked at his hands.

"The rave was several days ago, homie. Where's the spoils?"

"Danny Ames took it."

The color went out of Turtle's face. "Come again?"

"Danny Ames took it."

Turtle rubbed his face. He said, "Do you know how to use your phone? Phones are pretty amazing. You could have texted that to me and we wouldn't have bust in this motherfucker and been all rude to our host." He pointed at the coffee table. "May I?"

Charlie extended his hand.

Turtle did a line.

Little John did a line and yelled, "Holy cows!"

Turtle said, "Don't pay attention to him. Pay attention to me. He's a waterhead."

Little John said, "Better bring my floaties."

"So Danny Ames took the money."

Shane nodded.

"It was what…"

"I don't know. I didn't count it."

"We priced it out at about fifteen k. Would you say that sounds right?"

Shane thought about it. "Sounds right."

"Okay. So, do any of you have fifteen thousand dollars?"

Turtle looked at me. I shook my head. He looked at Charlie, who said, "This isn't my fuck-up. I didn't have shit to do with any of this."

Turtle nodded. "All right. Now, a part of me is wondering if there's not some subterfuge going on here."

Shane's eyes went wide.

"Hold on. I'm not done. You coming back here, just sitting there waiting to get fucked, that's not what guilty people do. So I believe you."

We all deflated a bit.

"But you still owe us." He turned to me. "How much do you have on you?"

I went into the guest bedroom and opened up the drawer. Brought them back around five hundred bucks.

"Don't you motherfuckers sell drugs?"

I told him, "Mostly I eat them."

"You ever heard 'The Ten Crack Commandments?'"

"Yes."

"Didn't take?"

"No."

Turtle and Little John stood up to leave. "It's like this, guys. Your buddy here hooked it up. And we'll subtract the four grand we were gonna give you guys. That puts it at ten-five. I don't want it from this little faggot, I want it from you, Shane. It was your job, and this is your fuckup."

Shane drummed his fingers lightly on his knees.

Turtle waved. "I'm being nice, but only because I hate Danny Ames even more than you do right now. Holler."

Little John said, "Don't holler in the house!"

They left.

Charlie held Shane in a bear hug. The tattooed man thrashed and screamed. Black gums bared.

I watched.

Shane calmed and eventually fell asleep.

Charlie got a blanket out of his room and covered his cousin sleeping there on the floor.

He said to me, "If you've got somewhere else to go, you'd better go there."

I slept in my car.

III

FALLING BACK INTO IT

Like that it was over.

I lived my whole life on a path and for a moment there I strayed. I lived low and found out that I wasn't equipped for it. Charlie didn't call me anymore. I lived in my car for a bit.

Shane disappeared.

I just kind of floated.

Then I decided to try life again.

At one point my wife and I fell back into it. I called her and sobbed into the phone and she told me to come back over. The dog was happy to see me. When I walked back into the apartment I could smell who I was. She showed me her paintings and we listened to the songs she'd had on repeat.

All the old nicknames and shorthand came back. I was learning how to speak again. There are hundreds of tongues out there but you only really speak when you've invented your own language.

After spending the night together talking about everything, she left for work early the next morning. I lay in bed looking at the Christmas lights strung up along the wall and everything there was heavy. I thought about the bed. I thought about when I used to wake her up with a song and she'd stay quiet til I fixed the coffee and we went our ways.

I took a shower.

I left.

I lucked out. A friend of mine was out of a roommate. She offered to let me stay for a month without rent. She had four Chihuahuas. I sat on her couch and played with the dogs and slept on an air mattress in the guest bedroom.

I walked back into the hot dog restaurant. I filled out an application and the owner read it over and said, "You look familiar."

I said, "I get that a lot."

"You don't look like you get that a lot."

I said, "I'm ready to work."

He said, "Well, we need a dish man."

"I am your dish man."

"Welcome aboard, dish man. Show up to work on time, and never fucking steal from me."

"Okay."

"If you steal from me, I'll kill you." He turned back to his laptop.

The steam from the dish pit left a layer of grime that I couldn't shower off. I pulled the accordion hose down and sprayed the pots and listened to music on my phone and cleaned the rubber mats. I mopped the floors and joked with the cooks. We smoked cigarettes out back and they talked about their kids and wives. We talked about which waitresses we'd fuck and exactly how we'd do it. I would laugh and watch the snow collect on the chairs out on the empty patio and I'd go back in and spray more pots. I'd scrub them with a wire brush. It gave me time to think.

I pushed down the door to the dishwasher and I learned to enjoy the sound of the water moving.

After work I'd buy a six pack and walk home. One night I was in the corner store and a woman in a caftan was talking to the beer through the glass. "You're so cold. Pretty. You're so pretty and cold." I grabbed my beer and she turned to me and adjusted her giant glasses and said, "I'm the heir to a concrete fortune."

"Can I have five bucks?" I said.

She looked back through the glass. "It's so pretty."

Netflix and Chihuahuas till I passed out.

Then I woke up and did it again. For a time, it was exactly what I needed.

HALF

I met my mother at Chili's. I brought her a Reese's peanut butter cup.

We ordered our food and talked.

Every time we met, she talked about my father. She told me that she should have known better. That of course he wasn't at the gym at that time of night. She told me about a swingers' retreat he took her to. All the porn. She talked about how she'd take him back now, but it was too late. New loves, new lives. She missed him. Last time they met up he touched her hair. Now they hadn't spoken in years.

When she talked about him, it filled me with a deep fear. Every young man fights the truth that he's half his father.

I told her about my job and my place and her face lit up.

"I was worried about you."

"I know."

"You're my boy. I can't have my boy being so sad."

I started crying into my fiesta chicken. She came around the table and gave me a hug.

FROG

A cook and I were on our break. We were smoking cigarettes out in front of the restaurant. Across the street, a bearded man in a suit fell off his bicycle. He cursed at it and picked it up and tossed it into the street.

The cook said, "Looks like Frog is back on the sauce."

"Why do they call him 'Frog'?"

"He hops from town to town. Is what he told me."

I watched Frog kick the bike. Cars backed up and honking.

The cook said, "He comes in every day. Weird little fucker. Told me he had pills of weed. Panhandles enough to get a margarita and then sings songs and plays his harmonica."

"I like harmonica."

"You're whiter than shit."

"That is true."

"A couple days ago he had that suit on and he had a Bible. Said he was going to church."

"Looks like he missed church."

"Looks like he went to church."

Frog stormed off down the street. Bike still out in the road.

We heard a noise and turned to look into the restaurant. The college kids were tanked, and this was their last stop after the bar closed.

A brolic in a polo picked up a scrawny dude and bodyslammed him through a table. The cook and I recoiled and made a sound.

I turned back to him. Thought about it a bit. I said, "I need to go back to college."

SHARA

I met a woman and for the first time in a while it felt natural. Her name was Shara. I asked her out like a normal human being and she said yes and we ate tacos and drank beer out of fishbowl margarita glasses.

I hadn't spoken much to anyone in a long time, but when I talked to her I got my language back.

On our second date, she asked me about my wife.

"You guys aren't divorced?"

"No."

"Why not?"

"Just haven't gotten around to it yet, I suppose."

"Do you two still talk?"

I didn't say anything.

"You can answer," she said. "You're still gonna get laid."

After our third date we stripped out of our clothes and hopped the fence into the apartment complex pool and it was so cold but we held each other. Our lips turned blue and the groundskeeper kicked us out and so we went back to the apartment and played with the

Chihuahuas and smoked with my roommate and fell asleep on my air mattress.

For our fourth date, I hung out at her place and she showed me an ayahuasca vine she'd ordered from the internet. We checked the internet for tips as to how to strip it and make tea, but we never did it.

I held her cats and my face itched something fierce, but I didn't mind.

She'd check her phone and tell me, "It's time for you to go. He's coming over."

I'd tell her we should fuck first.

She'd say, "He's literally on his way."

Then we'd do it frantically, quickly, and she'd shove me out the door with my pants still down.

The fifth time I saw her, I went to a party and we shared looks but said nothing. All the men at the party swarmed her.

We kissed behind a door quickly and she ran off.

Our sixth meeting, she gave me books to read. I met up with her and her man and their friends at a bar and we all laughed and carried on and I touched her leg under the table.

Seven was the park. We sat in the empty outdoor stadium on the stone steps and watched Renaissance Fair kids practice sword fighting.

Eight was when she told me that she couldn't be in a relationship, and she just had a need to explore and find out what worked for her, but that she couldn't tell her man because he wouldn't understand. She was torn that way: there was a wild life that she wanted and then this gravity, this man with feet firmly planted. So she did both. All of it. When she wanted.

I loved that she was that way. I loved that when we were together, we were best friends, but that when I left, there was someone else to be her best friend.

Our ninth date, she took me to a greenhouse. She named the plants for me. There was a tree in the greenhouse from Africa that only needed a few drops of water a year. "Any more than that, and it will die," she said.

We turned on music back at her apartment. We smoked a bowl. Laying in bed, she said, "We're all our own. That's all we can be."

I liked that.

I liked her.

My steps were light.

I had found the track.

Shane texted me on our tenth date. Shara and I finished up a game of minigolf. I told her about what to expect. Her eyes went wide. "We can roll tonight?" she said. "Let's fucking go."

ZARAGUIN

When we pulled up there were cars parked on the lawn. Bass rattling the house. Shara kissed me quick on the cheek and hopped out. I followed.

Charlie greeted us at the door.

"No Mustang," I said.

"Yeah, I finished it," he said. "I don't know if it's in much better shape, but the guy seemed happy. So whatever."

He handed us beers.

I saw Shane sitting on the couch. I sat down next to him. Shara wandered into the kitchen to mingle with the hoodrats.

Shane nodded at her. "Nice, man."

"Thanks."

"How have you been?"

I chugged half the beer. "I've been good, man. You?"

"Better. Things have been better."

Outside it began to pour sleet.

"How did all that shit go?"

"I paid them." And that was all he said on that.

He reached into his pocket and brought out two pills. "One for you, and one for your girl."

I examined the capsule. "It's brown."

"It's some new shit. Super pure. I'm feeling great."

I ate mine and got up and gave Shara hers and got another beer. Sat back down with Shane. He'd gotten more tattoos on his face. When he smiled they overlapped.

The pill kicked in.

We talked for a long time about this and that.

"So you wash dishes."

"I wash dishes."

"What's that like?"

"It's like. I don't know. It's like scrubbing pots."

"Scrubbing pots, right."

"And you?"

"I'm selling again. Back in my element."

"Elemental being."

"That's me."

The party kept up and two folks rap battled in the living room. We watched them. Shara hollered and threw her fist up and danced.

"She's a wild one," he said.

I nodded.

Shane told me, "I'm not sure if I'm ever meant to be happy. I thought a lot about what you said. About being the man who stops for stoplights. I started thinking about what we are here to do. And I think I know. I'm here to be a heathen. That's my thing. I can't be any other way. I'm on some howl-at-the-moon shit. I'm okay with that. But sometimes I wish I could get happy."

"You could."

"*You* could. You're built to be happy. It's just, the thing about people built that way. They don't know what to do when that's not the way it is anymore."

"I haven't felt happy in a bit."

"I think you have. I think you just live with it. So it's like, furniture. It just is. You don't know."

Shara sat down next to us. Shane said, "I can see your aura plain as day."

She crossed her legs and stared deep into him. "Yeah?"

"Yep. You're a bright red."

"And what does that mean?"

"Passion."

Charlie stumbled over to us and grabbed me by the arm and dragged me outside. We smoked cigarettes on the porch.

"So I've got this thing," he said. "Where Starburst, you know the candy right, Starburst will pay me to have a Caddy here at my place. They wrap the body kit in Starburst shit and they pay me to drive it around. I have this thing."

"That sounds cool."

"It is." He took his cell phone out. "Let me show you pictures of all the bitches I've fucked since I saw you last."

He showed me for fifteen minutes.

"That many?" I said.

He nodded. "It's been like a monsoon. But with, like, pussy juice."

I peeked in the window. Shane and Shara were still talking. She had her leg draped over his lap.

I thanked Charlie for the smoke and went back inside.

I said, "Well, I think it's about time for us to head out."

They didn't say anything.

Shara hopped up from the couch and took my arm and led me over to a corner.

"We're gonna go back in his room."

My guts turned. "All right."

She touched my face. "Want to come, too?"

The drugs made my face hot. I said, "Sure."

She went back to the couch and picked Shane up by the hand. She led us into the bedroom.

Shane stuck out his split tongue at me.

I smiled as best I could.

Shara kissed Shane, then she kissed me. Back and forth like that, and I measured the time between.

She got on her knees. Shane unbuckled his belt and his pants slumped to the floor. She sucked him off and I took my pants off and started pulling on myself, watching them. She pulled her lips off him and turned to me and looked up at me with these eyes and I wish I'd seen those eyes otherwise. She worked on me.

We got on the bed and Shara put me back in her mouth and Shane got in her from behind and we rolled like that. Her face turned red and Shane hit it so hard her forehead bumped into my stomach. She took some time to breathe and looked back at him and told him, "Holy fucking shit, yes," and then got back to me. I looked up at the spackle in the ceiling. Shane said, "I'm gonna come all over this ass," and then he pulled out and did it.

She looked back at the mess he'd made and arched her back and kissed him. She said, "I don't know if I've ever been fucked that hard in my life." I pulled her away and laid her on the bed. I began to sweat. Shane was catching his breath. She put her hand on my face and looked in my eyes and told me to come inside, but I pulled out and shot it over her belly.

We lay there on the bed, in the dark, smoking cigarettes.

They talked about this and that.

I stayed quiet.

We ate some more pills.

Shane stroked Shara's hair. She gripped her chest and shook gently. I thought he spoke. I was sure he spoke.

"Let me tell you how to be happy."

I was sure he said, "You're already feeling the week's death and rebirth on the horizon, and you wonder to yourself if this wasn't going to become a problem, like get exponentially worse, like one day you'll start mourning the death and rebirth of the day and then after that the death and rebirth of an hour and then maybe seconds and on and on. Seems like a totally not-chill way to live, right?"

I was sure he said, "Let me tell you how to be happy. Go outside and look up at the constellations and notice that there are two bees touching bright glowing stingers. Snap your fingers like 'oh yeah!' and go out to your garage where you keep your collection of bee stingers. Hopefully you've been collecting them steadily, as you are an adult, and have accumulated enough for the project at hand. Take a tube of superglue from the shelf and glue the stingers to each other, face up, until you form a little hollowed-out pyramid, about the size of a tent."

While the others shouted in the living room, while they tacked up blankets to keep the sun from peeking through the blinds, he said there in the dark, "Throw the bee-pyramid into the back of your Jeep and drive out into the desert and set the pyramid on completely flat land, where the cracks in the dirt look like wrinkles in a brain. Take off all of your clothes and feel that cool night air. Do a dance, whatever dance you like, but while you do it look up at the bee constellation, right where you left it, and shout at it, tell it that you don't want the week to die, that you're worried that you can feel your skin getting older, that the weight of thousands of invisible signals is making your brain heavy and saggy, that you want an answer, dammit."

While Shara breathed softly, while she arched her back and fought against the high, I was sure Shane said, "Retrieve the straight razor from the back of your trunk and cut out your tongue and let your mouth fill with blood, but do not break your concentration. You want answers, and now you're speaking the bee's language. Place your tongue in the middle of the bee-pyramid and continue to dance and inquire as to the nature of things until two bees appear before you, glowing radioactive green, their antennae touching. They will bend at the thorax and touch stingers and the stingers will meld together like two globs of paraffin wax in a lava lamp. At this point, the bees will begin to suck into each other, black eyes staring out in opposite directions, and if you wait until the two pairs of antennae connect and shrink like the last line of static stretched across a TV screen, disappearing to a point, if you wait until it gets to that point and you grab it, this floating green orb, and you put it in the dirt at your feet and spin a slow circle in the center of your bee stinger pyramid you will open a portal to the underworld. You'll float down softly and you will never remember the constellations and you will slide down a hollowed-out femur like a straw cut length-wise into a pile of bones and you will meet the scorpion loa, the Baron Zaraguin, god of assassins, and you can ask him what's coming, you can ask him but he won't say a word, won't read to you from the whiteboard hanging in the dark of his office."

While Shara quieted on the bed, I was sure he said, "He'll lower his stinger and you'll wrap your arms around it and he'll lift you up off the carpet of crushed bones to a green dot floating in the particle board of his ceiling, and you'll forget what it means, this green dot, but it will remind you of the lasers that would shoot from the stage you stood on when you were in the dreams of a popstar from Tokyo, and you will reach out to the crowd and let them sing the lyrics to the songs you've written, but every audience member is only a lonely minstrel by a fire in the woods, and you'll notice your hands, that they're your mother's hands, and that you are your mother, and you will meet your father as a young scared teenager and you will pass notes and you will walk home from the bus stop past the mailbox and then your head is through the green portal and you're asleep in the desert in your bee stinger pyramid, with a brand-new tongue and a whole lot of happiness, under constellations you've only just remembered existed at all."

They hollered and whooped out in the other room. They screamed and tore at their hair. But Shane just sat there in the dark with me. All the life was gone out of the space and the blinking clock on the nightstand, and I was sure the heathen said something.

ABOUT THE AUTHOR:

J David Osborne lives in Portland, OR with his partner and their dog. This is his third novel.

www.ingramcontent.com/pod-product-compliance
Lightning Source LLC
Chambersburg PA
CBHW032115280326
41933CB00009B/846
* 9 7 8 1 9 4 0 8 8 5 0 9 4 *